Longman

Great British Ghosts

Nick McIver

 LONGMAN

Addison Wesley Longman Limited
Edinburgh Gate, Harlow,
Essex CM20 2JE, England
and Associated Companies throughout the world.

First published 1982
Sixteenth impression 1996

Acknowledgements
We are grateful to the following for their
permission to reproduce the photographs: Nick
McIver for pages 2, 3, 5 and 21; the British
Tourist Authority for pages 7, 12 and 35; the
National Portrait Gallery for pages 13, 15 and
18 (inset); Photoresources for page 16; the
Museum of London for page 18; Lance Brown
for page 25; Robert Estall for pages 30–31;
Mary Evans Picture Library for pages 40 and
41; Peter Underwood and The Ghost Club
for page 43.

Illustrated by Paul Burbeck.

Produced by Longman Singapore Publishers Pte Ltd
Printed in Singapore

ISBN 0-582-53043-1

Contents

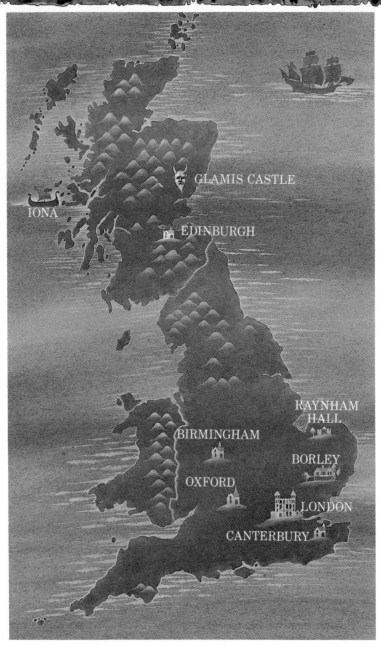

The ghosts that haunt these places are all in this book.

Do you believe in ghosts? Do you think that dead people come back to haunt the world?

This is a book about ghosts in Britain. It is a book about ghosts of today, and ghosts of the past. Some of the ghosts are famous, some of them are unknown.

What is the truth about ghosts? I have met and talked to several people who have seen ghosts. You will read some of the stories in this book. I believe that they were telling the truth.

This book does not try to explain ghosts. It just reports them.

Perhaps you don't believe in ghosts—yet. Read this book, and try to explain the stories in it. Then perhaps you will find that you *must* believe in them.

Ghosts in London

London is full of ghosts. No one has been able to count
the number of stories about ghosts in the city. These
ghosts do not only appear in famous old buildings like the
Tower of London. There are also haunted houses, pubs,
streets and theatres. There is a haunted tree in Green
Park, and ghosts appear in several London churches.

(Above) The haunted tree in London's Green Park

(Opposite) 50 Berkeley Square is a fine old house with a fearful past

The ghost of Berkeley Square

London has many beautiful squares. Berkeley Square,
with its trees and gardens, is one of the most beautiful.
50 Berkeley Square is an office today; it used to be a famous
haunted house. It was the home of a *very* nasty ghost.

Between 1870 and 1900, no one wanted to live in
50 Berkeley Square. There were too many noises at

night, and too many ghostly
appearances. At this time,
the people in the next house
used to wake up and hear
strange sounds—footsteps,
bangs and crashes—
nearly every night.

A young English lord,
Lord Lyttleton, stayed in
the house one night.

"I don't believe in
ghosts!" he told his friends.
"I'm not frightened.
I'll stay in the house."

In the middle of the night,
the people in the next house
heard the sound of a gun.
Next morning, Lord
Lyttleton came out of the
house with a look of terror
on his face.

"Something came into
the room," he said.
"I fired my gun at it,
but nothing happened.
The house *is* haunted, and
I'll never stay there again."

3

But there is another, more famous story about
50 Berkeley Square.

Two sailors arrived in London in 1875. They were
looking for work on a ship, and they had no money and
nowhere to sleep. They were walking round London, and
they came to Berkeley Square.

One of the sailors saw Number 50 and said, "Look!
There's an empty house. We can sleep there."

So they went into the dark and empty house, and
climbed the stairs.

"I don't like it in this house," one of them said. "It's
cold and dark and . . . frightening."

"Don't be a fool, man!" the other answered. "We had
nowhere to sleep, and now we've found this nice house.
Let's stay here."

They went into a bedroom at the top of the house, and
soon they were asleep. In the middle of the night, they
both woke up—suddenly.

"Ssh! Listen!" one of them said. "I can hear something.
There's someone downstairs."

"Yes," said the other. "I can hear footsteps . . . and
they're coming upstairs!"

At that moment, the door opened slowly . . . very
slowly . . . and "something without a shape" came in.
One of the sailors was too frightened to move. He just sat
there, and watched the terrible "thing".

The other ran out of the room, down the stairs, and out
of the house. He found a policeman, and together they
returned to the house. The sailor was too frightened to go
in, so the policeman went upstairs to the bedroom alone.

There was no one there!

He looked in all the rooms, upstairs and downstairs,
but he couldn't find the second sailor. Then he looked
out of the window . . .

The sailor was lying in the garden. He was dead.

Did the sailor jump out of the window? Or did
"something" push him? We will never know.

The ghost at the Theatre Royal

The Theatre Royal is one of London's most famous theatres

One day, in 1848, some workers were mending the Theatre Royal in Drury Lane, a famous old London theatre. They pulled down a wall in the upper circle of the theatre, and found a small secret room.

On the floor in this room they found the skeleton of a man. A knife was sticking in the skeleton.

Who killed this man? When? And why?

Many people have seen a ghost at the Theatre Royal. They think that this is the ghost of the dead man in the secret room. Why? Because the ghost always disappears at the place that used to be the secret room—through the wall.

This ghost always wears the same clothes. He wears a grey coat, a hat and tall riding boots. He also carries a sword. In fact, he wears the clothes of an Englishman of about 1750. And he usually does the same things. He appears in a seat in the upper circle. Then he stands up, walks slowly across the theatre, and disappears into the wall. He always appears in the daytime, between 10 a.m. and 6 p.m. Usually actors and actresses see him when they are rehearsing a new play, or when they are doing an afternoon performance.

At one afternoon performance in 1950, the British actor Morgan Davies saw the ghost.

"I was acting in *Carousel* on a Saturday afternoon. In one part of the play I was on the stage for twenty-five minutes. I looked up into the theatre, and saw an empty box. When I looked again, there was a man in a grey coat in the box. He was standing up. Then he raised his arm—and I could see *through* it! I watched him for about ten minutes. Then he disappeared."

Another time, when actors were rehearsing a new play, there were about a hundred people on the stage. The ghost did his usual walk, from the seat in the upper circle into the wall, and seventy of the actors saw him.

And then there is the theatre cat! The cat goes to all parts of the theatre—but it will *not* go into the upper circle!

The Theatre Royal ghost does not try to talk to people, and he doesn't hear people who talk to him. But actors think that he is friendly.

"We like to see the ghost at Drury Lane," one actor said. "If he appears before the first night of a new play, people are going to like the play. A lot of people will come to see it. He has appeared before some very successful plays— *The King and I, My Fair Lady, Oklahoma* and *South Pacific* among them. But he never appears before an unsuccessful play."

(Opposite) The ghost only appears before successful plays

The ghost at Covent Garden Underground Station

The ghost at Covent Garden Underground Station has
something to do with the theatre, too. William Terriss
was a famous actor of his time. In 1897 he was acting in
a play at the Adelphi Theatre. One night he died in the
street outside the theatre—another actor killed him with a
knife. Just before he died, William Terriss said very
quietly, "I will come back!"

Many people believe that he does come back. Many
people have seen his ghost. It has walked in several different
places—in the Adelphi Theatre, in the street outside, and
in Convent Garden Underground Station!

Every night after the play, William Terriss used to
catch a train home from the station. His ghost still walks
there sometimes, people say. A busy station is an unusual
place to find a ghost, isn't it? But this station is not open
late at night or on Sundays. So the staff are often there
when it is empty.

One of the staff, Jack Hayden, worked there for nine
years. One night he was locking up the station. He looked
around: nobody was there. Then suddenly he saw a tall
man. The man was walking up some stairs. He ran after
him, and called out. When he got to the stairs, there was
nobody there.

A few days after that Mr Hayden was eating a meal in
the staff dining room. It was just after midnight. The last
train had gone, and the station was empty. Suddenly a
door opened, and the same tall man was standing there.
He stood and watched Mr Hayden. Mr Hayden could

see him clearly. He noticed his clothes. They were the clothes of about a hundred years ago. He was also wearing light-coloured gloves on his hands.

"What do you want?" Mr Hayden asked. "The last train has gone."

The figure didn't answer, and it moved away. Mr Hayden went after it, but when he got outside the door, again there was nobody there.

Four days after that, in the middle of the day, Mr Hayden heard a scream. Another worker at the station ran into the room. He was terrified. He said that he had seen a strange tall man with light-coloured gloves on. He walked towards the man . . . but the man disappeared in front of his eyes! The worker left his job the next day.

But the two men wanted to find out about the strange tall figure. They were certain that they had both seen the same man. But who was he? One day Mr Hayden saw a picture of William Terriss at the Adelphi Theatre.

"That's him! That's the man I saw," he thought to himself. So he asked the worker to look at the picture.

"Yes, that's him. I saw him very clearly. That's a picture of the ghost. He's wearing the same clothes!" the worker said.

This all happened in the 1950s. Since then, about twenty people have seen the ghost with the light-coloured gloves. Several people spoke to it, but it never answered. Mr Hayden says that the ghost usually appears in November and December. It often comes to the staff dining room. It just stands and watches the people for a moment. It often comes on Sundays, too, when there are no trains. When the station is empty, the staff have also heard footsteps along the train lines. The footsteps are always going towards the next station on the way to William Terriss's old home.

Why does the ghost of William Terriss haunt the station? Do you think he is trying to go home?

The station staff don't know, of course. But many of them never use the staff dining room.

The ghost at St Thomas's Hospital

St Thomas's is a hospital on the south side of the River Thames. There is a ghost at St Thomas's—the Grey Lady.

I have met one person who has seen the Grey Lady. Charles Bide was a workman at St Thomas's Hospital during the second world war. I met him in 1979 and he told me about the day that he remembers so clearly.

Question: Mr Bide, when did you see the Grey Lady?

Answer: During the war, in 1943. A lot of bombs were falling on London then. One day, a bomb fell near the hospital and blew down parts of one hospital building. The next day I went to that part of the building. I had to look for some furniture.

Question: What happened?

Answer: Well, I remember that it was a very cold morning. Very cold. I went into the building. I went up the stairs to the top floor. I began to look for the furniture. Then I saw a mirror on the wall. The room was suddenly much colder. Then I saw a . . . figure . . . in the mirror. She was behind me, but I couldn't turn round. I just looked at the figure in the mirror. I looked at her eyes. They were very sad . . . the eyes of a woman with no love in her life.

Question: What did you do then?

Answer: I just stood there. I was too frightened to move, and that's the truth. I stood, and looked into the mirror. Then, suddenly, I ran. I ran down the stairs, and out of the building.

Question: What did the figure look like?

Answer: She wore a grey dress, like the dresses that hospital nurses wore a hundred years ago or more. But . . . her eyes . . . her eyes frightened me. They were so sad. And the room was so cold. It was a cold morning, but the room was colder.

Question: Did you tell anybody about the ghost?

Answer: Yes, I told a doctor. He said: "Don't tell anybody. There's a war, and this is a hospital. We don't need stories about ghosts too. We've got enough trouble."

Question: Have you ever seen the Grey Lady again?

Answer: No, but I will always remember that one time. Other people have seen her, in or near the same place.

The Tower of London

The Tower of London—home of many famous ghosts

William the Conqueror, the first Norman king of England, ordered his men to build the Tower of London in 1078. Three and a half million people visited the Tower in 1978, nine hundred years later.

But how many visitors know about the Tower's ghosts?

There are many ghosts in the Tower. Let us look at just five of them—the ghosts of Anne Boleyn, Margaret of Salisbury, the two little princes and Sir Walter Raleigh.

Anne Boleyn

Anne Boleyn (1507–1536)

Anne Boleyn became the second wife of King Henry VIII in 1533. But in 1536, Henry wanted another wife, so Anne became a prisoner in the Tower. The same year, the executioner received an order to cut off her head on Tower Green.

Many people have seen Anne's ghost since then. Sometimes she appears with her head, sometimes without it. People see her in the church in the Tower; sometimes she is looking out of a window in the White Tower, and sometimes she is walking on Tower Green.

In 1846 a white figure came towards a guardsman late at night.

"Stop!" the soldier said, but the figure did not answer. So the soldier tried to bayonet the figure—but he was not successful: his bayonet went straight through! Other guardsmen have seen this white figure, and they all say that she has the face of Anne Boleyn.

But there is a stranger story about Anne Boleyn.

In 1972 a nine-year-old girl was visiting the Tower with her father. She wasn't a clever girl; she didn't know about Anne Boleyn, or Henry VIII, and she didn't think that the Tower was very interesting.

She and her father were in a party with several other visitors. A guide was showing them the Tower, and telling them about it.

The guide had shown them the White Tower and the Bloody Tower, and when they reached Tower Green, he stopped.

"Here," he said, "on Tower Green, some famous prisoners died. The executioner cut off their heads with an axe like the one that you saw in the White Tower."

Then he gave the names of famous people who had gone to execution there. The father noticed that his small daughter was very quiet, and she was looking very closely at the Green.

". . . and here, the executioner's axe also cut off the head of Anne Boleyn, Henry VIII's second wife," the guide said.

"Yes," said the little girl, suddenly. "I know. I've just seen her!"

The other visitors laughed, but the little girl continued: "But you're wrong about one thing. He didn't cut off her head with an *axe*, but with a *sword*!"

This was true. Anne Boleyn was a queen, so they brought a special sword from France for her execution. The girl also described other things about the execution—and all of them were true.

How did a little girl of nine know these things? Her father said: "She didn't read about it—she never reads books. And nobody told her."

The girl herself said: "It's easy. I saw it. We were standing on Tower Green, and I saw the whole execution."

Margaret Pole, Countess of Salisbury

Anne Boleyn's was not the only execution on Tower Green while Henry VIII was king (from 1509 to 1547). Margaret Pole's execution was perhaps the most terrible.

Margaret Pole, Countess of Salisbury, died at the Tower on May 27, 1541. Why? Because King Henry didn't like her. There was no other reason.

On the morning of her execution, this poor old woman— she was seventy years old—cried to her executioner: "Why do you want to execute me?"

He could not give an answer. So she ran away from him. He followed her, and tried to cut off her head. When he caught her, he hit her five times with his axe. Her head came off only after the fifth time.

Sometimes, on May 27, people see this terrible execution again. The old woman is running away from her executioner, and he is hitting her with his axe.

The two little princes

This window in Canterbury Cathedral shows the two little princes with their father (Edward IV) and mother

Perhaps the story of the little princes is the most famous story about the Tower of London. It isn't just a story: it really happened.

Edward V became king of England in 1483 when he was only twelve years old. His brother was only ten. Their father was dead, but they had an uncle, Richard. He was a very bad man, and he wanted to be king himself. So he killed both the princes. He didn't kill them himself, but he paid another man to kill them.

Richard was very friendly to the little princes. He was a "kind" uncle; he looked after them.

"I'll take the princes to the Tower," he told their mother. "They are very young. They will be safe in the Tower."

At that time the Tower was a palace as well as a prison. But their mother was frightened. She knew that Richard was a nasty man. But he was also a powerful man, and she couldn't say no to him. She let her little boys go to live in the Tower. She never saw the princes again.

The murder was secret, of course. Richard ordered Sir Robert Brackenbury, the keeper of the Tower, to kill the princes. He was in the quiet church in the White Tower when the order came. But Sir Robert was a good man.

"I will die myself," he said, "but I will not murder these royal children!"

So Richard found another man, Sir James Tyrell. He promised him money and power, and Sir James accepted. He thought it was an easy job. The little boys were asleep in bed when Sir James came quietly into their room in the the Bloody Tower. He held the bedcovers over the boys' faces. It was quick; there wasn't a sound.

After some time, people began to ask questions. "Where is the king? Why haven't we seen him?" Slowly, the terrible story reached people's ears—the secret came out. The English people knew that Richard had murdered their king and his brother. But nobody could find the bodies.

One night, a soldier was walking past the Bloody Tower. At the bottom of the staircase, he saw two children. They were wearing long white nightclothes. The older boy was holding the little one's hand. They didn't make a sound.

"That's very strange," the soldier thought to himself. "There aren't any children here . . ." And while he watched, the silent little figures disappeared. Then he knew . . . he had seen the ghosts of the little princes.

Almost two hundred years after the murder, in 1674, some men were working on the Bloody Tower. They dug into the ground at the bottom of the staircase. And they found the bones of two small bodies.

The murderer had been in a hurry. He had just put the bodies at the bottom of the Bloody Tower staircase, and covered them with earth and stones. And the soldier had seen the silent little ghosts just at that place. Perhaps they came to help people find their bodies.

People never forgot the murder of the princes in the Tower. Some people also say that the murder gave the Bloody Tower its terrible name.

Sir Walter Raleigh

Sir Walter Raleigh did not die in the Tower, but he was a prisoner there for a long time, from 1603 to 1616. Sir Walter was a favourite of Queen Elizabeth I; he was a brave sailor, and one of the most famous men of the Elizabethan Age. But Elizabeth died in 1603, and the new king, James I, did not like Raleigh. He sent him to the Tower as a prisoner.

Raleigh's life in the Tower was not a bad one. He had several rooms in the Bloody Tower. His family used to visit him, and sometimes stayed with him, and he had enough money for clothes and food.

He was very friendly with the officers at the Tower, and he used to have supper with the Lieutenant. In the

Sir Walter Raleigh (1552–1618) spent thirteen years in the Tower

evening, he used to walk from his rooms in the Bloody Tower to the Lieutenant's house.

They say that, on some nights, Raleigh still walks from the Bloody Tower. They say that you can see a dark figure on "Raleigh's Walk", between the Bloody Tower and the Lieutenant's house.

Anne Boleyn, Margaret of Salisbury, the two little princes and Walter Raleigh are only five of the Tower's ghosts. There are many more. There are cries in the night, ghostly figures—even the ghosts of animals.

If you visit the Tower in the daytime, with hundreds of other visitors, it is not easy to believe these stories. But would *you* like to spend a night, alone, in the Bloody Tower?

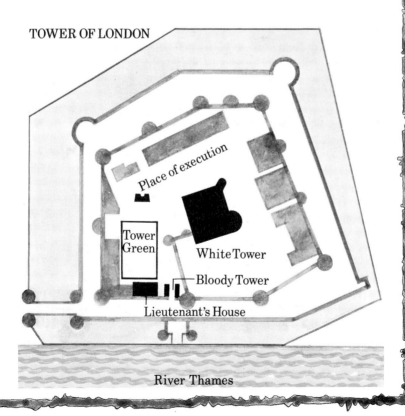

TOWER OF LONDON

Place of execution

Tower Green

White Tower

Bloody Tower

Lieutenant's House

River Thames

Borley—the most haunted village in Britain

About one hundred kilometres northeast of London, near the beautiful old town of Long Melford, you will find the village of Borley. Borley is on the top of a small hill; it is a very small village—just a church and a few houses.

In 1863 the Reverend H.D. Bull became priest at Borley church. He built a house, Borley Rectory, near the church, and he lived in it with his family.

When the Rev Bull died at the rectory in 1892, his son, the Rev Harry Bull, became priest at Borley Church.

On the evening of July 28, 1900, three of his young daughters—Ethel, Freda and Mabel—were returning home

to the rectory. They were nearly home when they saw a figure. It was a nun, and she was walking near the house. They could *see* the nun clearly, but her feet made no sound. The girls were very frightened, and Ethel ran into the house to fetch her older sister.

The older girl walked towards the nun. She wanted to ask "Who are you?", but the nun disappeared. One moment she was there, and the next ... gone!

Some people said: "Ah! The Bull girls aren't telling the truth. They're only children and they're making up the story."

But a doctor saw the nun, and a teacher, and in 1972

People have heard music in the empty church at Borley

a team of scientists saw her too. Were they all making it up?

Since 1900, the famous Borley nun has appeared to many people in the village. Who is she? No one knows. Some people think that this story is true.

Hundreds of years ago, there was a nunnery at Borley. A nun fell in love with a man from the village, and they wanted to leave Borley together. But the other nuns found out, and they killed the poor girl. Now, every year on July 28, the ghost of the nun returns and looks for her lover.

Some people say that the ghostly nun is about twenty; others say that she is older. But they all say that she is very sad.

The ghostly nun is not the only phenomenon at Borley. People have heard the sound of footsteps, and they have heard music in the empty church. Lights used to go on and off in the rectory, and furniture used to move.

The Rev Guy Smith moved to Borley Rectory in 1928. He didn't like the noises, the lights or the ghost, so he asked Harry Price to come to Borley. Harry Price was a famous "ghosthunter". He visited Borley many times between 1930 and 1939, and wrote books about the Borley phenomena.

In 1930 a new priest, the Rev Lionel Foyster, moved to Borley with his young wife Marianne. They were very friendly with Harry Price. At this time the Borley ghosts were very busy: doors locked themselves, furniture moved, lights went on, writing appeared on the walls. Harry Price wrote about all these things.

But now people say that Marianne Foyster was not telling the truth about the phenomena; they say that she wrote on the walls herself. They say that we cannot believe Harry Price's stories; that he made them up.

Maybe we cannot believe Marianne Foyster and Harry Price ... but there were phenomena at Borley *before* 1930 and *after* 1939. Can we believe *nobody* who saw and heard things at Borley from 1863 to today?

There was a fire at Borley Rectory in 1939, and it burnt the house completely. If you go to Borley today, you can still see the field the old house used to stand in. People still hear strange noises in that field, and the church is still haunted.

Perhaps there will always be ghosts at Borley.

Graveyards

Sometimes graveyards are very frightening places. There are many ghost stories about them. A lot of people are afraid to walk through a graveyard at night.

Lights at midnight

More than two hundred years ago, an English writer told the story of some ghostly lights in a graveyard. The lights appeared at midnight. They moved slowly between the graves, close to the ground. Then the lights went out, one after the other. People were very frightened. The first night, three people saw the lights. They screamed and ran away. The next night, several men went there to watch. They waited quietly. When midnight came, the lights appeared again. The men were very frightened. They left the ghostly place quickly. But one man stayed. He wasn't certain: were these ghosts or not? Suddenly he heard a quiet laugh behind him. *That* wasn't a ghost!

"Who's there?" he called. There was no answer, but he heard another little laugh. Someone moved in the bushes beside the graveyard.

"Come out!" the man shouted. "Come out of that bush!"

Slowly, three little boys appeared from the bush.

"What are you doing here?" the man shouted at them. "Go home!"

"Yes, sir. Sorry, sir. But—please . . ." the boys said.

"What?"

"Can we go and catch our tortoises, please?"

"Your *what*?" asked the man. He was very angry now.

"Our tortoises. They're . . . well, they're in the graveyard!"

The boys had played a joke to frighten people. They

(Opposite) A lot of people are afraid to walk through a graveyard at night

had put candles on the backs of some tortoises. Then they lit the candles and let the tortoises go. These were the "ghostly" lights in the graveyard!

"I don't think your joke is very funny," said the man. "I'm going to—" But the boys had already run away.

"Dead Man's Walk"

London has a famous haunted graveyard. Many years ago
the Old Bailey in London was the terrible Newgate Prison
—a name that brought fear to people's hearts. A high wall
ran along one side of it. The wall still stands there today.
Inside this wall was a narrow passage. This passage was
the prison graveyard. They used to put the bodies of the
prisoners there after execution. There was a metal walk
over the passage. Prisoners in chains used to walk along it
to their execution; their bodies lay under it afterwards. This
was "Dead Man's Walk"—a sad and terrible place. Of
course, this was many years ago. But sometimes, late at
night, people still see a ghostly dark shape on the high wall.
This terrible thing moves slowly along the top of the wall.
People also hear the sound of chains and the noise of heavy
feet along "Dead Man's Walk" in the middle of the night.
What is this horrible shape? Is the ghost of a poor prisoner
trying to climb over the wall? Nobody knows . . .

The gravestone cutter

Some stories about real ghosts are quite funny, too.
Perhaps ghosts like jokes sometimes. This is a modern
ghost story. It happened a few years ago near Oxford, in
England.

A young woman was walking home from work one winter
evening. She was walking through a graveyard. She wasn't
afraid: the graveyard was near her home and she knew it
well. But she was surprised that night. She could hear a
noise—tap, tap, tap. The noise went on, and she walked
towards it. Then she saw a man. He was working on one of
the gravestones. He was cutting the stone. He was spelling
the letters of a name on it. The woman stopped and
watched him. He looked up and smiled at her, but he
didn't speak.

"Why are you working now?" she asked him. "It's dark."

"Yes, I know," he said. Then he smiled again. "But
they spelt my name wrong."

A modern ghost

A lot of ghosts first appeared a long time ago. You do not often find a modern ghost—from the 1970s or 1980s.

This chapter is about a ghost that appeared in 1978, in a house in a town near Birmingham. This house was only about twenty-five years old; it wasn't a "strange" or "ghostly" house.

The family in this story are still alive. We shall call them the "C" family. There are Mr C, Mrs C, their daughter and their three sons. The youngest son was a baby in 1978. The daughter, Jane, was seventeen.

Here is the story, in Jane's words.

"We lived in the house from 1967 to 1978, and we were very happy there. It was always a nice, friendly house.

"Then, one night in June 1978, I suddenly woke up in the middle of the night. An old lady was standing near my bed. She was looking at me. I thought, 'I must be dreaming,' and I went to sleep again. The old lady was nice and friendly, and I wasn't frightened.

"I didn't think about it the next day. But a few days later, in the daytime, I saw the old lady again. She followed me around the house. She was walking, but her feet were about twenty centimetres above the floor.

"After that, I saw her nearly every day. I began to be very frightened, so I told my mother. At first she didn't believe me. She thought I was making it up. But then, a few days later, my mother saw her too. My mother was standing on the stairs, and she saw the old woman downstairs. The old woman went into the dining room. My mother ran downstairs and went into the dining room— but the room was empty! She, too, was very frightened.

"Other strange things happened. Sometimes we couldn't open doors, and at other times we couldn't shut them.

"Then, one night, my middle brother came downstairs, with a look of terror on his face. His bed and my oldest brother's bed were in the same room. He was asleep, but suddenly he woke up and heard strange noises from the other bed. He thought his brother was ill, so he went across to his bed . . . but no one was in it! My oldest brother was still watching television—downstairs!

"We told my father about these things, but he didn't believe us. 'You're being silly,' he said.

"But one night, the whole family was watching television. My boyfriend was with us, too. Suddenly we all heard loud noises upstairs. There was a bang and a crash. Furniture was moving about, and we could hear it. My father jumped up out of his chair. 'What's that?' he said. 'It must be a thief!' He ran upstairs and went into my bedroom. There was nobody in the room—but someone had put all the small pieces of furniture on my bed.

"My boyfriend was very frightened. He never came into the house again.

"In November 1978 we moved to another house. We didn't want to leave the old house; we liked it. But we didn't like the noises or the old woman.

"I went back to our old house once. I was standing just inside the front door. Suddenly the old woman was there. I didn't see her, but I could feel her. She put her hands round my neck, and threw me out of the front door. I can still remember those strong, ice-cold hands on my neck. I'm never going back there again."

This is a true story. The Cs now live happily in their new house. They don't see any old women, and they don't hear any strange noises.

Scottish ghosts

Scotland is possibly more famous for its ghosts than England. Scotland—with its old castles. Scotland—the home of the Loch Ness Monster. Scotland—with the winds that moan over the wild Scottish mountains.

Scotland is a good home for ghosts.

Glamis Castle

Glamis is one of the oldest castles in Scotland. Today it is the home of the Earl of Strathmore and his family. It is also the home of several well-known ghosts. None of them do any harm.

There is the Grey Lady, who often walks in the small church near the castle. Several people have seen her, and they all say that she is very quiet and very sad, and that you can see through her.

Some people think that she is the ghost of Janet, wife of the sixth Lord Glamis.
Janet was possibly a witch, and they say
that she tried to kill King James V of Scotland.
In those days they used to burn witches,
and in 1537 the king's men took Janet
to Edinburgh and burnt her.
Perhaps she has returned,
and haunts her old home?

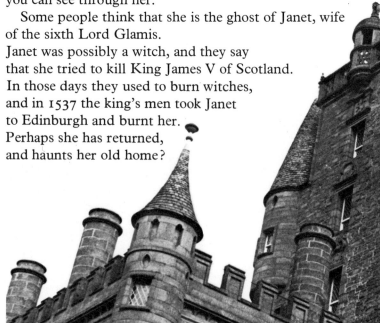

Then there is "Jack the Runner". Jack is a strange figure, but he never does any harm. He just runs across the park and into the trees when the moon is shining. Who is he, or who was he? Nobody knows.

There is also a ghost who appears and shows her red, bloody mouth to visitors. Some people say that she is the ghost of a servant who used to kill people and then drink their blood. Others say that an early Lord Glamis once cut out the tongue of one of his servants, and that this poor woman now haunts the castle.

The most famous stories from Glamis are the stories about Earl Beardie and about the Glamis "monster".

One dark night, in about 1450, Lord Glamis was playing cards with some friends in a tower of the castle. One of these friends was Lord Crawford. Crawford had a long black beard, so people called him "Earl Beardie". Beardie

Glamis Castle

was drinking a lot that night, and he was losing the game of cards. He was also getting very angry, and very nasty.

In the end, Lord Glamis said: "Beardie, you're getting too angry. Go away. We won't play with you any more."

Beardie got angrier. "You won't play with me?" he shouted. "Then I'll play with the Devil!"

At that moment, the door slowly opened and a tall figure—half-man, half-animal—came into the room. "So, you want to play with the Devil, do you?" he said to Beardie. Then he sat down and began to play cards. He beat Beardie, got up, and left the room.

A few days after this, Beardie died.

Since that night, many people have heard loud angry shouts from the tower, and some people have seen a man with a long black beard, always at four o'clock in the morning. The story says that there is a secret room in the tower, and the ghost of Beardie plays cards with the Devil there . . . again, and again, and again.

The second story is about the "monster" of Glamis Castle.

People say that, between 1800 and 1820, the Earl of Strathmore had a son. The baby was a monster. The family didn't want anybody to know about the boy, so they put him into a secret room.

The boy grew up, but he always stayed in the room, and the family always kept the secret. The monster died when he was more than a hundred years old, and the family never used the room again.

The monster is dead—but the story remains.

There is one other interesting story about Glamis. There is one more window *outside* the castle than there is *inside*. There is a window that you can see from outside the castle, but you can't find it inside. So there must be a secret room in the castle.

Perhaps the body of the Glamis monster is in this room? Or perhaps Beardie plays his game here with the Devil on dark, windy nights . . .

Edinburgh

Edinburgh is very different from Glamis. Glamis stands alone, far from any town. Edinburgh is a busy and beautiful city. A lot of visitors go to Edinburgh to see the castle, the good shops and the old buildings. But Edinburgh, too, has its ghosts. Perhaps the strangest was the ghost at 15 Learmonth Gardens, in the 1930s.

In 1936 Sir Alexander Seton and his wife went to Egypt. In Egypt, Lady Seton found a bone from an old Egyptian mummy, and she brought it back to Edinburgh, to their home at 15 Learmonth Gardens. Sir Alexander put the bone in a glass case on a table in the dining room.

After a few days, the Setons began to hear strange noises in the night. One night, the table in the dining room fell over . . . but no one was in the room.

A friend of the Setons was staying with them at the time, and he saw a "strangely dressed person" going up the stairs.

The servants didn't like these noises or strange figures in the house, so they all left.

Sir Alexander locked the bone in another room. That night, loud noises from that room woke him up. He jumped out of bed and ran into the room with his gun . . . but no one was there. Someone, or something, had moved all the furniture, and had thrown all the books on the floor.

Lady Seton wanted to keep the bone, but Sir Alexander said, "No, we mustn't keep it. The bone is haunted."

But where could he take it? He didn't want to sell it, and he didn't want to give it to anyone. In the end, he burnt it on the fire.

The noises stopped, the furniture didn't move any more and no one saw ghostly figures again. But Sir Alexander himself wrote: "I have not been happy since that day." This was true. Soon afterwards, Sir Alexander lost a lot of money, his wife left him and he was often very ill.

Iona

There are a lot of very beautiful islands near the west of Scotland. Iona is one of these islands. St Columba built a monastery on Iona in AD 563.

In December 986, a small army of Vikings from Denmark came to the island. They killed the monks, took their cows and sheep, and their gold, and burnt the monastery.

In 1950 an artist, John MacMillan, was staying on Iona. He was painting pictures of the island. One evening, he was walking near the old monastery. Afterwards he told a very strange story.

"I wanted to go and see my friend Mrs Ferguson. I often go and see her, and I know her house well. She lives very near the old monastery. But on this evening, I couldn't find her house. I know this is silly ... but her house just wasn't there!

"I thought, 'I *know* her house is here. I'm an artist—I've painted pictures of it! Perhaps I'm ill!'

"So I sat down. I was looking out to sea, when I saw fourteen Viking ships. They were coming towards the land, and I could clearly see the Vikings in the boats, and the pictures on the sails. I remember the pictures on the sails very well.

"The ships reached the land, and the Vikings jumped out. Some monks were working in the fields. They ran towards the monastery, but the Vikings caught them and killed every one of them. Then the Vikings ran into the monastery, and a few minutes later they came out and took gold, food and drink, and farm animals down to the boats. Then they burnt the monastery, and the boats went away.

"'I must be dreaming,' I thought. 'First I can't find the house—and then I see all these Vikings.'"

When he got home, he sat down and painted the Vikings and their boats. He also painted, very carefully, the pictures on the sails of the boats.

A few weeks later, he took these pictures to the British Museum in London. A man from the museum studied the pictures.

"Ah!" he said. "This is very interesting. You are a good artist, Mr MacMillan, but where did you see these pictures? These are Viking pictures from about AD 950 to 1000!"

So the Vikings came to Iona in 986—and an artist "saw" them in 1950.

John MacMillan is not the only person who has "seen" the Vikings, but his story is the most interesting. He not only *saw* the Vikings—he *painted* them as well.

Orchard End

Sometimes you can go into a house and say, "Something is wrong with this house." A close friend told me that he had lived in a haunted house. But this was a haunted house without white figures, strange old women, or bloody ghosts. It was an "unhappy" house—and strange things used to happen ...

"In 1960 my father and mother moved to a new house. I was twelve years old at the time. The house, *Orchard End*, was a 1930s' building, not big but not very small. It stood in a large and beautiful garden in the country near Canterbury.

"We knew that there were stories about the house, and about the people who had lived in it. A rich businessman had lost all his money while he was living there. Another man had died very suddenly. He was still young, and he had lived in the house for only nine months.

"But *Orchard End* was beautiful, and my family liked it very much.

"I soon noticed that something was wrong with the house. Every Thursday, my mother went out to the shops, and I stayed in the house by myself. I didn't feel happy on those Thursday afternoons. I wasn't an easily frightened child ... but I felt that there was 'something' in or near the house.

"One Thursday afternoon, I was reading a book. Suddenly, I saw someone; a man was walking past the window at the side of the house.

"'That's strange,' I thought. 'There's someone in the garden.' But I wasn't afraid. I thought, 'It must be a visitor. I'll go and talk to him.'

"So I went to the door, opened it, and waited. But no one came! I went to the side of the house, and I went into the road. But there was no one.

"Then I *was* frightened. Someone had been in the garden—and now he wasn't there! I ran out of the house, and waited for my mother at the bus stop.

"Then there were the noises in the night. Often, when I was lying in bed, I heard footsteps. They came up the stairs, and towards my room. I used to think, 'Ah, it's Mother.' But then . . . no one appeared.

"My mother and father heard these noises too. Soon we began to laugh about it. We used to say 'Ah! There's the ghost again!' But we were not happy. My father lost his money, and I was not successful at school.

"I left school, and left home. My mother and father continued to live there. Then, suddenly, my mother became ill and died, at the age of fifty-four. I returned to *Orchard End* for a few months.

"One night, at about ten o'clock, I was leaving the house in my car. This always took a long time. I had to drive to the gate, open the gate, drive the car out, and then shut the gate again. This night, I drove to the gate, and got out. Suddenly, I heard a voice.

" 'Shh! Be quiet!' the voice said.

"I jumped, and looked round. I could just see a young girl, about seventeen years old, I think.

" 'Who are you?' I said. 'Where have you come from?'

" 'Be quiet,' she answered. 'Don't tell them I'm here.'

"I thought, 'This is very strange, but perhaps the girl is playing games with some other young people.' So I said, 'OK, I won't tell them you're here.' But I looked up and down the road, and I couldn't see anybody. I drove the car out of the gate, and got out to shut the gate.

"In those few moments the girl had disappeared! She wasn't there! She hadn't gone into the garden—I knew that. And she wasn't in the road—I could see that there was nobody for a hundred metres.

" 'Who was she?' I asked myself. 'Where did she come from? Was she real, or have I seen a ghost?'

"My father moved to another house a few years ago. He is happier now. I have never seen other people who appeared and disappeared."

Seeing is believing

In all the stories in this book, people say that they have
seen or heard ghosts. But we don't know that the stories
are true: we haven't seen the things ourselves. Anybody
can tell a story. But people say that the camera can't lie.
So, if a ghost is in a photograph, it must be real. Do you
believe this? Can anybody photograph a ghost? Many
people have tried. There are several famous ghost pictures
on these four pages.

About a hundred years ago, people loved photographs of
ghosts. There were hundreds of "spirit photographs".
Some old photographs of ghosts are very silly. They aren't
real: you can see that they are fake. You can explain them
easily, too. The photographer has printed the picture twice,
with one negative on top of another. Photographers used
to do this often. Then they could sell their pictures for a
lot of money.

But there are modern pictures of ghosts, too. They are

(Opposite) This "spirit photograph" is about a hundred years old

(Above) The Brown Lady of Raynham

41

more interesting.

Several famous people saw the ghost of the Brown Lady at Raynham Hall in Norfolk. In 1936 a photographer and his assistant went to take some photographs of Raynham Hall. When they were putting up their cameras at the bottom of the staircase, the photographer saw a strange white shape. It was at the top of the stairs. The shape became the figure of a woman, and moved slowly down the stairs.

"Look! What's that?" the photographer cried.

"What?" asked his assistant. "I can't see anything."

The photographer quickly took a picture. The assistant laughed at him. "There's nothing there," he said.

But when they printed the picture, the ghostly shape of a woman's figure was clear. Many people have looked at the negative of this photograph carefully. They all say that it isn't a fake.

Many people don't believe in the "ghosts" in these photographs. But some very strange things have appeared on film. The picture on page 43 is perhaps the most interesting. Nobody can explain this photograph. Look at it carefully. How many figures can you see on the staircase? One figure is clear, and you can see the arm and hands of another figure above him. Look at the hands —they are holding the stair rail. You can see the figures clearly, and you can see the rings on the fingers, too. Here is the story of this ghostly picture.

In 1966 a Canadian tourist and his wife visited the Queen's House at Greenwich in London. This beautiful house is over three hundred years old. Part of the house is now a museum. People go in and out all the time. The tourist, the Reverend Hardy, took this photograph of a staircase in the Queen's House. His wife was with him. When he took the picture, the staircase was empty. The light was shining on the staircase, and *there was nobody there*. But when they saw the photograph afterwards, the ghosts were there.

Can you explain this photograph of the Greenwich ghosts?

The Reverend Hardy and his wife don't believe in ghosts. He certainly didn't try to make a fake picture. And he used a kind of film that you can't print at home. The firm that makes the film has to print it. And he couldn't take one picture on top of another: that's not possible with his camera.

So what happened? Nobody knows.

The Hardys sent the photograph to the Ghost Club in England. The Ghost Club keeps a large amount of material about ghosts—stories, pictures and material of all kinds. They try to find out about every story and every "ghost". The Hardys' picture was very interesting, of course. Nobody had seen a ghost at the Queen's House before this. There wasn't a famous ghost like the Brown Lady at Raynham Hall.

Several people from the Ghost Club went to the Queen's House one night. They stayed at the bottom of the staircase all night. They watched and listened; they had special cameras, film cameras and tape recorders for sound. The museum's photographer was with them. He took many photographs that night. But nobody saw the ghostly figures in the Hardys' picture. They *did* hear footsteps late in the night. Where did these strange footsteps come from? They didn't know. People who worked at the museum had heard them, too.

And you, have you ever heard or seen a ghost? Now that you have read this book, do you believe in ghosts? Write and tell me what *you* think.